Each Puffin Easy-to-Read book has a color-coded reading level to make book selection easy for parents and children. Because all children are unique in their reading development, Puffin's three levels make it easy for teachers and parents to find the right book to suit each individual child's reading readiness.

Level 1: Short, simple sentences full of word repetition—plus clear visual clues to help children take the first important steps toward reading.

Level 2: More words and longer sentences for children just beginning to read on their own.

Level 3: Lively, fast-paced text—perfect for children who are reading on their own.

> *"Readers aren't born, they're made.*
> *Desire is planted—planted by*
> *parents who work at it."*

> —**Jim Trelease**, author of
> *The Read-Aloud Handbook*

PUFFIN BOOKS
Published by the Penguin Group
Penguin Books USA Inc., 375 Hudson Street, New York, New York 10014, U.S.A.
Penguin Books Ltd, 27 Wrights Lane, London W8 5TZ, England
Penguin Books Australia Ltd, Ringwood, Victoria, Australia
Penguin Books Canada Ltd, 10 Alcorn Avenue, Toronto, Ontario, Canada M4V 3B2
Penguin Books (N.Z.) Ltd, 182–190 Wairau Road, Auckland 10, New Zealand

Penguin Books Ltd, Registered Offices: Harmondsworth, Middlesex, England

First published in the United States of America by Viking Penguin, Inc. 1987
Simultaneously published in Puffin Books
Published in a Puffin Easy-to-Read edition, 1994

1 3 5 7 9 10 8 6 4 2

LIBRARY OF CONGRESS CATALOGING-IN-PUBLICATION DATA
Ziefert, Harriet.
Mike and Tony: best friends / Harriet Ziefert;   pictures by
Catherine Siracusa.   p.   cm.   –(Puffin easy-to-read)
Summary: Best buddies Mike and Tony enjoy doing everything
together, from playing baseball to riding bikes, so their argument
over a pillow fight keeps them apart for only a short while.
ISBN 0-14-036853-1
[1. Friendship–Fiction.]   I. Siracusa, Catherine, ill.
II. Title.   III. Series.
PZ7.Z487Mi   1994   [E]–dc20   93-25617 CIP   AC

Puffin® and Easy-to-Read® are registered trademarks of Penguin Books USA Inc.
Printed in the United States of America

Reading Level 1.8

Mike and Tony: Best Friends

Harriet Ziefert
Pictures by Catherine Siracusa

PUFFIN BOOKS

Mike and Tony
were buddies.

They walked
to school together.

They ate lunch together.

Mike picked Tony
for his team.

And Tony picked Mike.

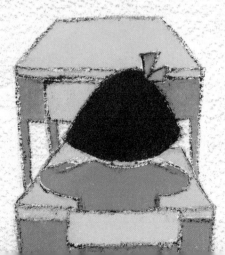

After school
they played ball...

and tag...

and leapfrog.

Sometimes they rode bikes.

And sometimes they did nothing much at all.

Every Friday night Mike and
Tony had a sleep-over.

They took turns
getting cookies.

They took turns calling
their friends on the phone.

One Friday night
Mike and Tony had
a pillow fight.

It was a small pillow
fight that grew...

and grew...

and grew!

Mike and Tony threw
down their pillows.

They grabbed each other
and wrestled.

Mike sat on Tony.

And Tony sat on Mike.
He yelled, "I win!"

Mike shouted, "You did not!
You cheat!"

Mike took his sleeping bag
and ran out the door.

Tony called his mother.
"Mike ran away!"

"Let's go find him,"
said Tony's mother.

Mike was still mad.
He yelled, "You didn't win!"

Tony said, "Okay! Okay!
I didn't win. Nobody did."

Mike and Tony
were buddies again.